THIS BOOK
BELONGS TO:

....

....

The *Spectacular* TALE OF PETER RABBIT

"We would not be going *to the Fair. We would be* passing *it."*
Benjamin nodded...

THE *Spectacular* TALE OF
PETER RABBIT

BY

Emma Thompson

ILLUSTRATED BY

Eleanor Taylor

FREDERICK WARNE

FOR WILLIAM

FRIEND

SURVIVOR

TURKEY

– E.T.

FREDERICK WARNE

UK | USA | Canada | Ireland | Australia | India | New Zealand | South Africa

Frederick Warne is part of the Penguin Random House group of companies
whose addresses can be found at global.penguinrandomhouse.com.

www.peterrabbit.com

Penguin
Random House
UK

First published 2014
This edition published 2015
001

A CIP catalogue record for this book is available from the British Library

Printed in China

ISBN: 978-0-723-29989-9

Dear Reader,

This is the third story I have penned for Mr. Rabbit, whose thrill-seeking nature remains undimmed, even at an age where most of us prefer to put our paws up with a cup of tea and a digestive biscuit.

Conscious as ever of the fact that he enjoys sailing close to the wind, I have sent him upon an adventure which I trust will keep him happy, if not quiet, for some time.

Prepare for the spectacular
the particular
the fun-funicular
of the Fair!

EVER YOUR DEVOTED SERVT

- E. T.

IT WAS high summer and Peter Rabbit had a cold.

He lay on his back in a patch of dry moss, looked up at the clouds and sneezed.

He was bored.

Just then, as if carried on the breeze, he heard the faint sound of a drum and pipes.

Peter sat up.

A TRAVELLING fun-fair had come to the village.

It had a coconut-shy, a Punch and Judy, a merry-go-round, a small roller-coaster and a sign which said "Everyone Welcome!"

EVERYONE
WELCOME!

PETER RABBIT and Benjamin Bunny were forbidden to attend.

"*A fair attracts the Feckless and Shifty,*" warned Mrs. Rabbit.

"*Instead, you may go and help Cousin Lupin pick his blueberries.*"

THEY set off and, somewhat lowered in spirits, stopped by the ford to nibble at a bank of sorrel.

On the breeze came the rooty-toot-toot of the pipes.

THEY both sat bolt upright and looked at each other.

After a moment, Peter said, *"It is just as well to reach Cousin Lupin's by the village road as by the hill."*

Benjamin nodded.

"We would not be going to the Fair. We would be passing it."

Benjamin nodded again.

As THEY neared the village green, Peter and Benjamin took very great care not to be seen.

But the visitors at the Fair were having far too much fun to notice two little rabbits squeezing through a hole in the fencing!

AT FIRST, the yelling and the laughing and the banging of drums were too much for Benjamin, who had to pull his ears down round his chin.

But Peter was *thrilled*.

His eyes grew rounder and rounder as he watched a man shooting pellets at tin ducks.

"*I WANT ONE!*" cried his little girl.

She pointed to the row of stuffed toys in front of the shooting gallery.

There were monkeys and bears and cats and dogs and mice, dressed in all manner of waistcoats, trousers and jackets.

Benjamin Bunny stared and stared. Their boot-button eyes stared back without blinking.

THE crowd jostled to see the man shoot for his little girl.

One of the toys, a cross-eyed kitten in a pink ruff, was knocked off the shelf.

Quick as a flash, Benjamin Bunny pulled it away and sat on it.

No-one saw.

A GREAT cheer went up!

The man had shot three ducks in a row!

A smiling stall-holder said to the little girl,
"Choose a toy, my dearie! Any one you like!"

The girl clapped her pudgy hands with glee,
looked at each toy carefully and picked up…

PETER!

He had been so still, watching in his blue jacket, that she had mistaken him for a prize!

He found himself being kissed all over and hugged so tightly he was nearly choked.

Then he was stuffed without ceremony into a small woollen bag.

BENJAMIN watched it all with rising horror.

Hardly knowing what he was doing, he began to follow the little girl, skittering from beneath one stall to the next, and dragging the cross-eyed kitten by its leg.

THEY reached the roller-coaster.

Benjamin could see Peter's ears swinging about as the father lifted his daughter into one of the waiting waggonettes.

As for Peter, once he had recovered from the shock, he took care to resist his natural urge to wriggle out of the bag.

Through the handles, he could just see the criss-cross beams of the roller-coaster as the waggonette began to rise.

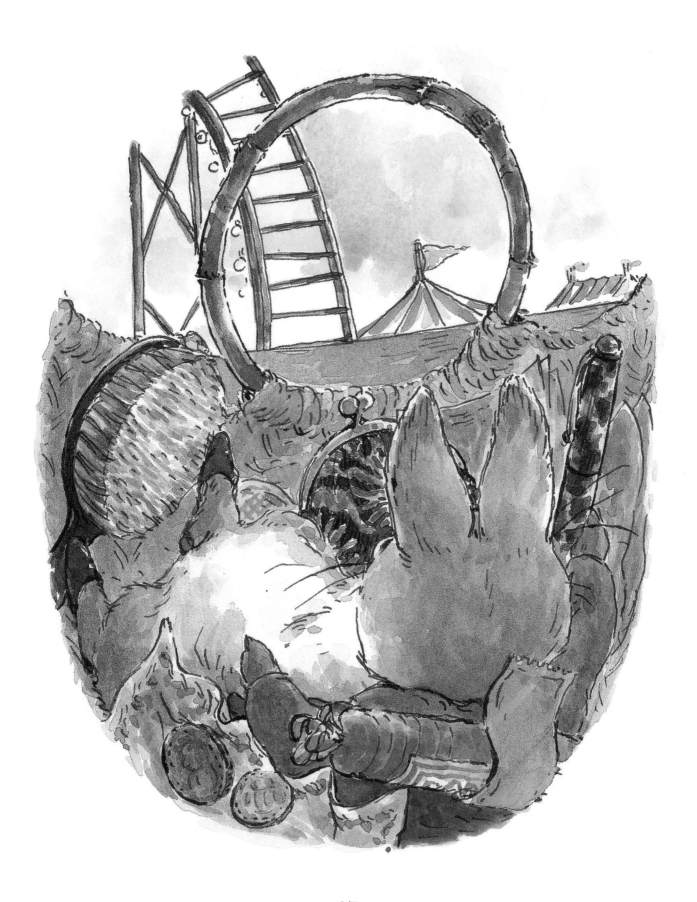

BELOW, Benjamin chewed on the kitten's tail to calm his nerves.

The waggonette seemed to clank upwards for a very long time.

Then suddenly it stopped.

FOR a dizzying moment
it teetered on the brink
and then

D

    O

        W

           N

                it plunged!

FROM the ground, all Benjamin could
see were Peter's ears billowing out of
the top of the bag.

"*Oh, my, my, poor cousin!*" he whimpered.
"*Whatever will become of him?*"

DODGING deftly under the stripey skirts of a red-faced lady selling toffee apples, Benjamin ran to the foot of the roller-coaster and hid inside a greasy poke of newspaper, which, judging by the smell, had recently contained fish.

AT THE same time, the waggonette containing the father, his daughter and Peter came to a juddering halt.

The little girl skipped out, joggling Peter in the bag, which had become very oppressive.

Her father tried to follow but was less nimble.

"Me knee's stuck!" he roared. *"Help me, Flossie!"*

THE LITTLE girl dropped her bag on the ground and ran to help her father, laughing at his grumpy face.

Fast as lightning, Benjamin shot over, pulled Peter from the bag and put the cross-eyed kitten in his place.

THE cousins ran, although Peter, being wobbly in the legs, had to lean on Benjamin.

They reached the safety of the newspaper poke just in time.

For the little girl had picked up her bag and was looking with fury at the cross-eyed kitten.

"THAT's *not my TOY!*" she cried.

"Who's taken my toy?" She pulled out the kitten and threw it on the ground.

"Leave it, Flossie," said her father. *"Let's have a turn on the merry-go-round!"*

But the little girl refused to hear, her blue eyes darting here and there, swift and sharp as a hawk's.

Then Peter stumbled on an apple core.

One of the brass buttons on his jacket caught in the sunshine.

"*There!*" shouted the little girl. "*There's my toy!*" And she pointed directly at Peter and Benjamin.

THE rabbits froze.

The father looked over and frowned.
He rubbed his eyes.

*"I didn't win two of the blooming things,
did I?"* he muttered.

Then the girl rushed towards Peter.

Peter and Benjamin ran faster than they had ever run in their lives.

They shot past the coconut-shy,
  under the Punch and Judy,
    through the merry-go-round,
      WHICH WAS STILL MOVING,
and, unable to find the hole in the fencing,
simply ran directly out at the gate, past the
astonished ticket-seller.

THE little girl tried to keep up but was no match for two frightened rabbits.

She plopped to the ground and set up a wail.

"*Come now, Floss,*" said her father, tired of the Fair, the heat and the crowd.

"*One toy's as good as any other.*" And he handed her the cross-eyed kitten.

IT WAS an exhausted, filthy pair of bunnies, both smelling of grease and old fish, who tumbled on to the floor of the sandy burrow later that evening.

Mrs. Rabbit took one look at their tired, guilty faces and thought it prudent not to exact any punishment.

INSTEAD, they were bundled into a hot bath, rubbed vigorously with rough towels and put straight to bed with cups of hot milk and nutmeg (for its calming properties).

Peter couldn't sleep.

In the wee, small hours, Benjamin found him staring out at the fairground lights, which twinkled merrily on the dark horizon.

"Couldn't you have waited to rescue me until after the merry-go-round?" said Peter.

Benjamin simply pulled his blanket up over his ears.

THE END

ENJOY
THE *Further* TALES OF
PETER RABBIT

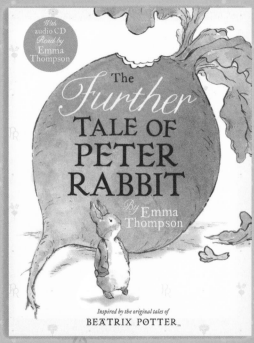

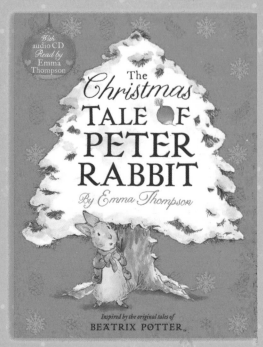

Paperback and CD
ISBN: 978-0-72326-909-0

Paperback and CD
ISBN: 978-0-72329-368-2

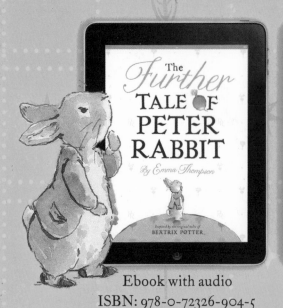

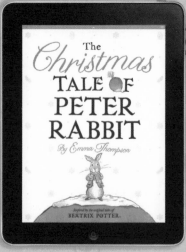

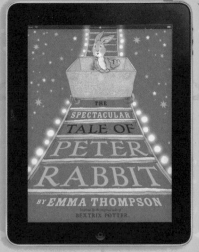

Ebook with audio
ISBN: 978-0-72326-904-5

Ebook with audio
ISBN: 978-0-72329-405-4

Ebook with audio
ISBN: 978-0-72329-754-3